Lion at School
and Other Stories

Lion
at School
and Other Stories

by Philippa Pearce
illustrated by Caroline Sharpe

Greenwillow Books, New York

Text copyright © 1971, 1977, 1979, 1985 by Philippa Pearce
Illustrations copyright © 1985 by Caroline Sharpe

The following stories were originally written for radio and published
as part of the BBC *Listening and Reading* series: "Lion at School"
(1971), "The Great Sharp Scissors" (1977), "Hello, Polly!" (1977),
"Runaway" (1979), "Secrets" (1979).

Printed in the United States of America
First American Edition   10 9 8 7 6 5 4 3 2 1

Library of Congress Cataloging-in-Publication Data

Pearce, Philippa.
Lion at school and other stories.
Summary: A collection of nine stories about animals,
including a lion who goes to school, a lonely horse in
search of adventure, and a mouse trying to avoid a mousetrap.
1. Children's stories, English. [1. Animals—Fiction.
2. Short stories] I. Sharpe, Caroline, (date) ill. II. Title.
PZ7.P3145Li 1985   [E]   85-17588
ISBN 0-688-05996-1

Contents

Lion
at School

Once upon a time there was a little girl who didn't like going to school. She always set off late. Then she had to hurry, but she never hurried fast enough.

One morning she was hurrying along as usual when she turned a corner and there stood a lion, blocking her way. He stood waiting for her. He stared at her with his yellow eyes. He growled, and when he growled, the little girl could see that his teeth were as sharp as skewers and knives. He growled: "I'm going to eat you up."

"Oh, dear!" said the little girl, and she began to cry.

"Wait!" said the lion. "I haven't finished. I'm going to eat you up UNLESS you take me to school with you."

"Oh, dear!" said the little girl. "I couldn't do that. My teacher says we mustn't bring pets to school."

"I'm not a pet," said the lion. He growled again, and she saw that his tail swished from side to side in anger—*swish! swash!* "You can tell your teacher that I'm a friend who is coming to school with you," he said. "Now shall we go?"

The little girl had stopped crying. She said, "All right. But you must promise two things. First of all, you mustn't eat anyone; it's not allowed."

"I suppose I can growl?" said the lion.

"I suppose you can," said the little girl.

"And I suppose I can roar?"

"Must you?" said the little girl.

"Yes," said the lion.

"Then I suppose you can," said the little girl.

"And what's the second thing?" asked the lion.

"You must let me ride on your back to school."

"Very well," said the lion.

He crouched down on the pavement and the little girl climbed onto his back. She held on by his mane. Then they went on together toward the school, the little girl riding the lion.

The lion ran with the little girl on his back to school. Even so, they were late. The little girl and the lion went into the classroom just as the teacher was calling the register.

The teacher stopped calling the register when she saw the little girl and the lion. She stared at the lion, and all the other children stared at the lion, wondering what the teacher was going to say. The teacher said to the little girl, "You know you are not allowed to bring pets to school."

The lion began to swish his tail—*swish! swash!* The little girl said, "This is not a pet. This is my friend who is coming to school with me."

The teacher still stared at the lion, but she said to the little girl, "What is his name then?"

"Noil," said the little girl. "His name is Noil. Just Noil." She knew it would be no good to tell the teacher that her friend was a lion, so she had turned his name backward: LION—NOIL.

The teacher wrote the name down in the register: NOIL. Then she finished calling the register.

"Betty Small," she said.

"Yes," said the little girl.

"Noil," said the teacher.

"Yes," said the lion. He mumbled, opening his mouth as little as possible, so that the teacher should not see his teeth as sharp as skewers and knives.

All that morning the lion sat up on his chair next to the little girl, like a big cat, with his tail curled around his front paws, as good as gold. He didn't speak unless the teacher spoke to him. He didn't growl; he didn't roar.

At playtime the little girl and the lion went into the playground. All the children stopped playing to stare at the lion. Then they went on playing again. The little girl stood in a corner of the playground, with the lion beside her.

"Why don't we play like the others?" the lion asked.

The little girl said, "I don't like playing because some of the big boys are so big and rough. They knock you over without meaning to."

The lion growled. "They wouldn't knock ME over," he said.

"There's one big boy—the very biggest," said the little girl. "His name is Jack Tall. He knocks me over on purpose."

"Which is he?" said the lion. "Point him out to me."

The little girl pointed out Jack Tall to the lion.

"Ah!" said the lion. "So that's Jack Tall."

Just then the bell rang again, and all the children went back to their classrooms. The lion went with the little girl and sat beside her.

Then the children drew and wrote until dinnertime. The lion was hungry, so he wanted to draw a picture of his dinner.

"What will it be for dinner?" he asked the little girl. "I hope it's meat."

"No," said the little girl. "It will be fish fingers because today is Friday."

Then the little girl showed the lion how to hold the yellow crayon in his paw and draw

fish fingers. Underneath his picture she wrote: "I like meat better than fish fingers."

Then it was dinnertime. The lion sat up on his chair at the dinner table next to the little girl.

The lion ate very fast, and at the end he said, "I'm still hungry, and I wish it had been meat."

After dinner all the children went into the playground.

All the big boys were running about, and the very biggest boy, Jack Tall, came running toward the little girl. He was running in circles, closer and closer to the little girl.

"Go away," said the lion. "You might knock my friend over. Go away."

"Shan't," said Jack Tall. The little girl got behind the lion.

Jack Tall was running closer and closer and closer.

The lion growled. Then Jack Tall saw the lion's teeth as sharp as skewers and knives. He stopped running. He stood still. He stared.

The lion opened his mouth wider—so wide that Jack Tall could see his throat, opened wide and deep and dark like a tunnel to go into. Jack Tall went pale.

Then the lion roared.

He roared and he ROARED and he **ROARED.**

All the teachers came running out.

All the children stopped playing and stuck their fingers in their ears. And the biggest boy,

Jack Tall, turned around and ran and ran and ran. He never stopped running until he got home to his mother.

The little girl came out from behind the lion. "Well," she said, "I don't think much of *him*. I shall never be scared of *him* again."

"I was hungry," said the lion, "I could easily have eaten him. Only I'd promised you."

"And his mother wouldn't have liked it," said the little girl. "Time for afternoon school now."

"I'm not staying for afternoon school," said the lion.

"See you on Monday then," said the little

girl. But the lion did not answer. He just walked off.

On Monday the lion did not come to school. At playtime, in the playground, the biggest boy came up to the little girl.

"Where's your friend that talks so loudly?" he said.

"He's not here today," said the little girl.

"Might he come another day?" asked the biggest boy.

"He might," said the little girl. "He easily might. So you just watch out, Jack Tall."

Runaway

One day Jim woke up feeling ill.

Jim's mother had to go to work. She didn't know what to do. Jim couldn't go to school, and he couldn't stay at home all by himself. In the end Jim's mother got him out of bed and put on his zip-up bedroom slippers for him and put on his duffel coat over his pajamas and put a rug around his shoulders and walked him around to Mrs. Pratt's house. Mrs. Pratt used to mind Jim before he was old enough to go to school.

Jim's mother knocked at Mrs. Pratt's front door. Mrs. Pratt opened it. She looked surprised and rather cross to see Jim in his bedroom slippers and his pajamas.

Jim's mother said, "He's not well enough to go to school."

Mrs. Pratt said, "I can't look after him today. I'm doing all my washing today."

"Oh, *please!*" said Jim's mother.

"Well," said Mrs. Pratt, "he'll have to be very good and not get in my way."

"He'll be as good as gold," said Jim's mother. "He's not himself at all. He doesn't feel well enough to be bad."

So Mrs. Pratt agreed to mind Jim, and Jim's mother went off to work.

Jim lay on Mrs. Pratt's settee, still in his bedroom slippers and duffel coat, with the rug over him. He listened to Mrs. Pratt's washing machine. In the middle of her washing Mrs. Pratt came to ask if he'd like a cup of tea and some alphabet biscuits. She would make sure there were three biscuits that spelled J-I-M.

"No, thank you," said Jim, as polite as polite and as good as gold. Mrs. Pratt tucked the rug around him and went off again. She was kind when she wasn't worrying about her washing.

He listened some more to Mrs. Pratt's

washing machine, and he dozed off.

When he woke up, he remembered about the tea and biscuits, and wished that he hadn't said no. He felt hungry now. He felt better. In fact, he felt quite well again.

He got off the settee and went to look in the kitchen. Mrs. Pratt had just finished her washing. She was on her hands and knees, cleaning up a lot of water on the kitchen floor. She was muttering to herself. She sounded cross again. She didn't see Jim.

Jim tiptoed past the kitchen door and looked into the backyard. Mrs. Pratt's clean washing was hanging on the washing line, blowing in the wind. Jim went into the yard to

stand with the clean sheets and shirts and
other things blowing about him. One of Mr.
Pratt's shirts flapped its arms at him, teasing
him. He tried to catch the shirt. It twisted
away from his hands and flapped high in the

air, out of his reach. But in the end, of course, it had to flap down again.

"Got you!" said Jim.

The shirt pulled away from his grip. Jim hung on. The shirt gave a jerk, and Jim gave a big jerk back, just to show it.

And then, in a sudden hurry, the shirt rushed down on him, and all the other washing rushed down as well—right down to the ground. Jim had pulled the washing line down;

all the clean washing lay there on the dirty ground.

Jim was scared at what he'd done. He knew how very cross Mrs. Pratt would be. He scuttled back into the house—but quietly. He scuttled quietly past the kitchen door. Mrs. Pratt had just finished cleaning the floor. She was beginning to stand up. Then she would look out of the kitchen window into the backyard.

Jim didn't wait for Mrs. Pratt to look out of the window. He ran to the front door, and out of it, and went running down the street.

He ran and he ran and he ran. He ran himself out of breath. Then he stopped for a moment to look behind him: no Mrs. Pratt. So he
walked on, but quickly. He thought he knew
the way home. Certainly it wasn't far. When
he got there, he could sit on the doorstep and
wait for his mother to come home from work.
If Mrs. Pratt came looking for him, he could
hide behind the dustbins.

As Jim walked along, a car overtook him
and stopped. It had POLICE written along the

side. A cheerful voice through the window said, "Hello, sonny! Where are you off to in your bedroom slippers and pajamas?"

Jim ran. He ran and he ran, and he dodged down an alley for pedestrians only, where the car marked POLICE couldn't follow him. He heard the policeman shouting "Hi!" behind him.

He ran out of the alleyway and into an ordinary street. He ran and he ran and he ran. He ran himself out of breath again. Then he stopped to look behind him: no policeman.

The policeman in the police car must have spotted him because of his zip-up bedroom slippers and his pajamas. Jim noticed that people in the street sometimes stared at him, too. Well, he couldn't do anything about his bedroom slippers, but he stopped in a quiet place to roll up the legs of his pajamas. He rolled them both right up, so that they didn't show underneath his duffel coat anymore.

Then he went on, and

people seemed not to look at him so much.

He had given up the idea of going straight home because by now he had no idea where home was. His home couldn't be far away, but all the same Jim was lost. He didn't like the idea of being lost. He tried not to think of it.

He came to a street he did know: Market Street. There were stalls on either side of Market Street, selling fruit and vegetables and fish and meat and china and dress materials and old magazines and junk of all kinds. Jim had often been to Market Street with his mother. She did most of her shopping here, on her way home from work.

Today, as usual, Market Street was crowded. People with shopping bags went to and fro along the pavements and in the road between the market stalls. They filled Market Street, so that there was no room for cars to drive down it. There would be no danger to Jim from a car marked POLICE.

So Jim turned down Market Street. He walked past stalls selling fruit and all kinds of other food. He felt very hungry indeed, but he had no money to buy anything.

He went slowly on.

Now it began to rain.

Jim put up the hood of his duffel coat, but water was beginning to soak through the soles of his zip-up bedroom slippers. He thought to himself that he could keep dry if he crept under one of the stalls. He must do that.

But which one?

He decided on a fruit stall where there was nobody but an old lady choosing some bananas. He stood by the stall. The old lady was looking for the particular bananas she wanted. Jim moved right against the front of the stall. The old lady pointed upward to where her particular bananas hung, and the stall keeper looked upward to where she was pointing. No one at all was looking at Jim. He stooped quickly and lifted the sacking hanging over the front of the stall and crept underneath.

Underneath the stall was like a dim cave, with some of the space taken up by empty orange boxes and other rubbish. From a box at the far side of the cave there came a long, bad-tempered growl.

There was a dog.
A watchdog.

Jim nearly went back by the way he had just come, but he knew he might very easily be caught. He decided just to keep as far away from the dog as possible and be always ready to make a dash for it. As Jim's eyes grew used to the gloom, he could see the dog. It was very old and very fat. It didn't like Jim's being there, but it couldn't be bothered to get up and waddle across to bite him. There was nothing for Jim to do but sit quietly and try not to annoy the dog.

Jim found a pile of old sacks and settled into it. He sat and watched the feet of the

people passing on the rainy pavement outside. It might have been cozy for him in his nest of sacks if he hadn't been lost and hungry and thirsty.

Sometimes the feet on the pavement stopped at Jim's stall. He could hear the voices of the people buying fruit from the stall keeper. Fruit! Jim thought longingly of the fruit in the stall just above his head: apples, oranges, pineapples, pears. His mouth watered. In the cave under the stall there was nothing for Jim to eat, nothing for him to drink. The dog was luckier. It had a bowl of water just under its nose, and during the afternoon the stall keeper's hand came under the sacking with a meaty bone for it.

In the end Jim fell asleep on his sacks, and he dreamed that he was at home. He dreamed that his mother had made him pancakes for

tea. He'd put sugar on the first one, and his mother was saying something about lemon to go with the sugar. . . .

He woke up, and there he was on the sacks, and there were the feet of people passing to and fro on the rainy pavement outside, and somebody had stopped at his stall to buy fruit. He stared and stared at a pair of feet standing there—a woman's feet. Then, suddenly, he heard his mother's voice, almost over his head: "Yes, a lemon, please. Just one lemon. Yes, that lemon will do."

It was Jim's mother—really and truly his mother!

Jim burst out from underneath the stall, the watchdog barking furiously behind him. He flung himself upon his mother. His mother cried out, and all the shoppers round about exclaimed, and the watchdog waddled out and bit someone, which made the confusion worse.

Jim began to explain to his mother, but in the middle of explaining, he burst into tears because he was so hungry and thirsty—and lost. Then the fruit stall man brought him a cup of tea from somewhere, and someone else

gave him a bun to eat, and a junk stall man dug out a very old push chair and Jim's mother put him into it. The junk stall man put a moth-eaten hearth rug over Jim's knees to keep him warm, and his mother pushed him home. Jim had not been in a push chair since he'd grown big enough to go to school, but he didn't mind today.

When they got within sight of home, there was Mrs. Pratt, who looked more worried than she ever looked about her washing, and she had been crying, too, and there was the car marked POLICE as well. Everyone had a lot to say, but Jim's mother took Jim straight indoors and upstairs. She gave him a bath and put him to bed. Then she brought him his tea in bed; it was pancakes with lots of sugar and lemon.

Jim's mother told him how silly he had been to run away from Mrs. Pratt's and how very silly he had been not to let the police help him and bring him home. But she didn't tell him all that until after he had eaten four pancakes with sugar and lemon.

And after that he slept and slept and slept.

Brainbox

Once upon a time a horse lived by himself in a large meadow. His name was Brainbox, but he was not really a clever horse at all. In his meadow Brainbox had grass to eat and a stream to drink from, but he had no company. He felt very lonely. He needed another horse to be his friend.

One day Brainbox could bear his loneliness no longer. He trotted to the far end of his meadow; then he turned and began to canter, then to gallop toward the other end. He galloped as fast as he could—faster and faster— until he reached the hedge, and then he JUMPED. He cleared the hedge, jumping right

out of his meadow altogether and into the lane on the other side.

This is a lane, said Brainbox to himself. *If I go along it, perhaps I shall find another horse to be my friend.* He began to trot down the lane. As he went, he kept a sharp lookout for another horse.

One thing was worrying Brainbox: He was not certain of recognizing another horse if he saw one. He had lived alone in his meadow for so long that he could not remember what other horses looked like. *And if I can't remember that,* said Brainbox to himself, *then*

I've nothing to go on, have I? He was not a very clever horse.

He was not clever, but he was determined. *I shall just have to ask,* said Brainbox. *Ask and ask and ask again.*

The first creature he saw in the lane was a snake—a harmless grass snake. The snake was gliding among the grasses at the side of the lane.

Brainbox called, "Wait, you there!"

The snake paused a moment.

"Are you a horse?" asked Brainbox. "Because I'm looking for a horse to be my friend."

The snake gazed at him in amazement. "Sssssilly—sssso ssssilly!" hissed the snake. "Can't you see I'm not a horse? I'm a snake."

"How can one tell the difference?" asked Brainbox.

"Horses have legs, for one thing," said the

snake. "Snakes haven't—they don't need them. Watch!" And legless, the snake glided swiftly away and out of sight among the grasses.

"Well, now, that's a useful bit of information, for a start," said the not-so-very-clever Brainbox. "Now I know that I have to find a creature with legs if I'm to find a horse to be my friend."

And he trotted on down the lane.

The next creature he saw in the lane was a hen who had strayed from her hen run. She was pecking about in the lane when the horse caught sight of her. She pecked here at a seed, there at an insect, and as she pecked, she ran to and fro. *On legs!* said Brainbox to himself. So he called out, "You there, with the legs! Are you a horse? I'm looking for a horse to be my friend."

The hen cackled, "Bad luck! Bad luck! Bad luck! I'm a hen, not a horse, can't you see?"

"But you've legs!" said Brainbox.

"And I've wings, too—look!" said the hen, and she stretched her wings and flapped them. "Hens have wings; horses haven't."

"No winged horses?"

"No. Hens, yes; horses, no."

"Pity," said Brainbox. He thought: *This question of wings or not-wings complicates everything.* He decided not to think about wings or not-wings but to concentrate only on legs.

Aloud he said to the hen: "All the same, you could be a horse, couldn't you? You have legs."

"But only two," said the hen. "Hens have two legs; horses have four legs. Hens, two legs; horses, four legs. Hens, two; horses, four."

"So I need an animal with four legs if I want a horse to be my friend?" said Brainbox. He just wanted to check.

But the hen had seen a beetle in the grass. Without waiting to answer, she scuttled away after it, and Brainbox was left alone.

Four legs . . . he said to himself. He decided that he was sure he was right, even without the hen's saying so. *Four legs* . . . he repeated, memorizing the information. *Four legs . . . four legs . . .*

He began once more to trot down the lane.

The next animal he came upon was a dog who had just found an old bone. The dog was gnawing his bone, so Brainbox had time to look at him closely. Brainbox saw that the dog had legs. He counted them: one, two, three, four.

"I say!" he cried joyfully. "You've four legs—I've counted them! Exactly four! So, please—you are a horse, aren't you? I'm looking for a horse to be my friend."

The dog almost fell over with laughing; he even dropped his bone. Then he began barking madly at Brainbox: "Wruff! Wruff! Stuff and nonsense! Of course, I'm not a horse. I'm a dog—a dog—a dog!"

"But you've four legs," argued Brainbox. "Why shouldn't you be a horse?"

"My legs are dogs' legs," said the dog. "Quite different from horses' legs. For one thing, dogs' legs end in paws—look, like mine! Horses' legs end in hoofs, like yours. Legs with hoofs, that's what you want." And the dog picked up his bone and went off elsewhere to gnaw it undisturbed.

I'm getting a more exact picture, said Brainbox to himself. *I must find a creature with legs, four of them, and hoofs at the end of the legs. Then I've found a horse to be my friend.*

And he trotted off down the lane.

Farther down the lane he met a sheep who was wandering up it, browsing on the wayside grasses as it went. When the sheep heard the horse coming, it lifted its head to stare.

Legs, said Brainbox to himself. *And one, two, three, four of them. And each ends in— yes, in a little hoof!* He said aloud to the sheep, "Please, tell me, aren't you a horse? You've legs—four of them—and four hoofs as well. Surely you're a horse? I want to find a horse to be my friend."

The sheep stared and stared. Then it said, "Baaaaa! Baaaarmy—that's what you are! I'm a sheep, not a horse!"

"But your legs have hoofs!"

"Not like a horse's hoofs. Look at my hoofs."

"I did," said Brainbox, "when I counted your legs."

"Now look at your own hoofs."

"Why should I look at my own hoofs?"

"You're a horse, aren't you?" said the sheep.

"What's that got to do with it?" said Brainbox, confused.

The sheep stared and stared. It bleated something to itself which Brainbox did not catch. Then it said, "A sheep's hoofs are cloven. A horse's hoofs aren't." And the sheep turned its back on Brainbox and began browsing again.

Well, said Brainbox, trying to cheer himself up, *I'm getting nearer all the time. Legs; four of them; hoofs at the end of the legs; hoofs not cloven. Find all that, and I've found a horse to be my friend.*

And he trotted off down the lane.

Farther down the lane he met a donkey. They looked at each other. The horse saw that the donkey had legs. He counted them: one, two, three, four. He looked at the end of each leg: a hoof. He looked at the hoofs: uncloven.

Then Brainbox shouted at the donkey, "At last! You're a horse! And I've been looking for a horse to be my friend."

"Eeeyore! You're a fool!" said the donkey. "I'm a donkey, not a horse."

"But you have everything," Brainbox insisted. "Legs, four of them; hoofs, uncloven. *Why* aren't you a horse?"

"I've told you," said the donkey. "Because I'm a donkey."

Brainbox could have cried with disappointment. He stood, baffled and woebegone, in

the middle of the lane, his head drooping almost to the ground in his despair. He did not know what to do next.

In the end he begged the donkey to listen to the sad story of his search and advise him, and the donkey agreed. Then Brainbox told him all about his meeting with the snake and the hen and the dog and the sheep and their helpful remarks. "So you see," said Brainbox, "I thought I could *work out* what a horse would look like. At least I'd got the legs right."

"There's a lot more to a horse than a set of legs," said the donkey.

"I daresay," said Brainbox, "but I don't

know anymore. It all comes back to the fact that I've quite forgotten what other horses look like. I've got nothing to go on."

"You've something to go on," said the donkey. "You are a horse."

"Someone else said that to me," said Brainbox, puzzled. "They seemed to think it made a difference in some way."

"It does," said the donkey. "You know what another horse will look like."

"What will it look like?"

"Like you."

Brainbox was thunderstruck. "Like me . . ." He turned the idea over in his mind: It was new; it had possibilities; it might work.

"For instance," said the donkey, "look at your tail. Then look at mine."

Brainbox looked over his shoulder at his tail and swished it. He looked at it carefully, as he had never bothered to do before, and saw that his tail was made up of a great number of very long, strong hairs. Then he looked at the donkey's tail: It looked rather like an old-fashioned bellpull, with just a tuft of hairs at the end.

"Yes," said Brainbox, "I can see that our tails are quite different." He looked at the rest of the donkey and then at as much of himself as he could see. He said, "I don't look very much like you at all, except perhaps for the legs."

"It's not just looks either," said the donkey. "A horse will have a special voice, just like your voice; and he'll have a special horse smell, just like yours; and—and—well, when you meet another horse, you'll *know* he's a horse just because you're a horse, too."

"And you think I really might meet another horse?"

"I do," said the donkey.

"Then I'd best be off again," said Brainbox. "Thank you very much indeed for your advice." And he began trotting down the lane, in the direction from which the donkey had just come.

"Eeeyore!" the donkey called after him. "You're going to be lucky!"

Brainbox wondered what the donkey meant.

At the end of the lane Brainbox came to a five-barred gate. A creature stood on the other side of the gate, with its head hanging over the top bar, looking sad. Brainbox saw that the creature was four-legged, with un-cloven hoofs, and a tail of long, strong hairs. But it wasn't just the creature's looks that ex-cited Brainbox. The creature's smell was pleasantly familiar, and just when Brainbox was wondering what the voice would sound like, the creature lifted his head, looked straight at Brainbox, and said, "Neigh! neigh! The name's Dobbin. What's yours?"

"Brainbox," said Brainbox. "I'm a horse, and I *know* you're a horse, too. Why do you look so miserable?"

Dobbin said, "I live alone in this meadow, and I feel very lonely sometimes. There's no other horse to be my friend."

"Wait there!" said Brainbox. He turned around and began to trot back up the lane, the way he had come.

The donkey, who saw him approaching, called out, "You're going in the wrong direc-tion!"

"No, I'm not," said Brainbox. "You wait and see."

He trotted on past the donkey and then past the sheep and past the dog and past the hen and past the grass snake. They all stopped what they were doing to stare when they heard the sound of horse's hoofs approaching.

When he judged that he had gone far enough, Brainbox turned and began to trot back toward the five-barred gate at the end of the lane. He trotted faster and faster—

past the grass snake,

past the hen—

—faster and faster, until he was cantering—

past the dog,

past the sheep—

—faster and faster, until he was galloping—

past the donkey, who shouted, "Hooray!"—

—galloping—galloping—galloping—

till he came to the gate with Dobbin leaning over it—

"Mind out!" shouted Brainbox, and Dobbin drew to one side, and Brainbox JUMPED. He went sailing over the five-barred gate into the meadow.

"I've come to live here," said Brainbox to Dobbin. "To be your friend."

"Good," said Dobbin. "Very good indeed." He kicked up his heels for joy, and so did Brainbox. Then they galloped around the meadow together. When they were tired, they settled down to standing side by side, head to tail. Brainbox swished his tail to stop the flies from settling on Dobbin's head, and Dobbin swished his tail to stop the flies from settling on Brainbox's.

The two friends lived together in their meadow, keeping each other company, for many, many years. They were happy horses.

The
Executioner

A little old house stood alone, remote among the hills. It was a holiday cottage; people came to stay there just for a fortnight's holiday. There was a stream they could paddle in or swim in, or they could fish in it, and there were the hills to climb and wander among.

At the end of their fortnight the holiday-makers went home, and another lot came.

One fortnight Andy came with his mother and father and aunt and uncle and cousins. The little old house was filled with their noise and movement. But at night, when everyone was asleep, the little old house was still and

quiet again. It was still and quiet in the daytime, too, if the weather was fine and people went out.

Toward the end of Andy's fortnight, the weather was very fine indeed, and everyone went for picnics, bathed, fished, walked, climbed. They were hardly indoors at all in the daytime. The little old house was left to itself: empty, still, and quiet.

On one of the last days of the holiday Andy went on a long picnic walk with the others. The sun was very hot. Perhaps the sun was too hot for Andy, or perhaps the picnic food was too much for him. Whichever it was, he began to feel sick and dizzy. He felt really ill.

So his father took him piggyback all the way home and put him to sleep on his bed upstairs.

He drew the curtains to darken the room for Andy.

He said, "I shall be downstairs for a bit. Then I might go and fish in the part of the stream you can see from this bedroom window. You'd be able to see me if you drew the curtains to look out. You'd be able to call me if you wanted me, and I'd come. All right?"

"All right," said Andy, drowsing already.

Andy slept most of the afternoon and then woke slowly. He was alone in the little old house, so still, so quiet. A fly buzzed between the bedroom curtain and the windowpane; that was the only sound to be heard.

At last he decided to get up since he felt better. He drew the curtains back and looked out, and there was his father at the stream, as he had said he would be, still fishing.

Andy was dressed except for his shoes, and he did not bother to put those on again. In bare feet he padded downstairs and into the living room of the little old house. He flopped down into one of the armchairs.

Really he wasn't fully awake yet. He looked sleepily about him. There was the table, with the chairs ranged round it, where they ate their meals. Soon it would be teatime. The others would be back for tea. The mugs were already out on the sideboard.

He would have liked a mug of tea now, hot, with milk and lots of sugar, but he supposed he would have to wait for the others.

He'd just sit here and wait.

Still as a statue of a boy in a chair, he sat in the still, quiet room in the little old house.

Then, out of the corner of his eye, he thought he saw something move. Only a little movement, like a leaf stirring, but there were no leaves here indoors, on the floor.

He was startled, almost afraid. He twisted his body to look properly. His body moved, the chair creaked, and the movement he thought he had seen was over.

There was nothing now, yet he was sure he had seen something.

He went on looking. He stared and stared at the floor in front of the sideboard where he had surely—*surely*—seen something moving. And then he saw the movement again.

A mouse.

A mouse ran out from underneath the sideboard and paused in the middle of that patch of floor and looked at Andy steadily with tiny black currant eyes.

They stared at each other. Neither moved. Neither made a sound. Then the mouse went. Vanished under the sideboard again.

Andy never moved. He breathed softly, shallowly, so that his chest rose and fell as little as possible. He stared. He watched, staring.

The mouse was there again. Dark gray-brown; neat—more than neat: beautiful. Very small but solid, real, and yet with the speed of a moving beam of light.

Now it flickered under the table.

Found a crumb.

Ate it.

Flickered again.

Vanished under the sideboard.

This time the mouse did not return. In a moment Andy heard what the mouse had already heard: his father tramping back from his fishing. His father was pleased to find Andy downstairs and so much better. He put the kettle on for tea because the others would soon be back.

They all came back, and the little old house was filled again with their movement and

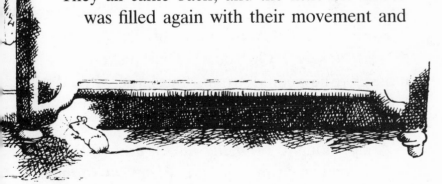

noise. They had bought two huge paper bags of currant buns from a shop in a village. Now everyone sat up at the table and drank mugs of tea and ate buttered buns. The buns were fresh and crumbly, and a good many crumbs fell on the table and some fell on the floor.

Andy looked at the crumbs on the floor and thought: *They won't still be there tomorrow morning.*

He was right.

The next morning, when he came downstairs to the living room, he looked at the floor: not a currant or a bun crumb to be seen anywhere.

That day Andy's aunt went to fetch the last of the potatoes from their basket on the floor in the larder. She came back, crying, "The potatoes have been gnawed!"

Andy's mother went into the larder and looked closely. "Oh, dear! That must be a mouse!" She peered around the larder. "And I think I can see the mousehole it comes from."

Andy thought: *And the larder door is old and doesn't fit to the ground. Plenty of room for a mouse to go to and fro between the larder and the living room.*

Andy's father said briskly, "What we need is a mousetrap." It was his turn to go to the village to buy provisions, and at the same time he bought a mousetrap. He brought it home with him.

Andy and his cousins had not seen a mousetrap before. This one had two little prongs on which Andy's father stuck a piece of cheese. This was the bait to entice the mouse to the trap. There was also a strong metal spring and two metal bars. All the metalwork of the trap was mounted on a flat piece of wood, a little smaller than a postcard. On the wood was written the name of this kind of mousetrap: THE EXECUTIONER.

Now Andy's father showed how the trap worked. He had already baited it and set it. He took a twig from the stick box by the fireplace. He pretended that the twig was a mouse. He dragged at the cheese with the end of the stick. His movement released the spring, and that snapped a metal bar down— WHAM! The metal bar snapped down with such force that it broke the twig right in half. "And that would be the end of the mouse," said Andy's father.

"I hate mousetraps," said Andy, and he went upstairs and lay down on his bed and tried to think of nothing at all.

That evening, before they all went to bed, Andy's father baited the mousetrap and set it and put it on the larder floor near the potatoes.

And when everyone was in bed, and all the lights were out, Andy crept downstairs. For a light he used his little pocket torch that his mother had given him in case he needed to go to the toilet in the middle of the night.

It seemed to be the middle of the night now, and the little old house was very still and very quiet.

Softly, softly, in the living room, Andy took a stick from the stick box, as his father had done. Then he tiptoed to the larder and opened the door and shone his torch inside.

There was the mousetrap, with the cheese in place.

And there, on the far side of the mousetrap, facing the mousetrap, was the mouse. It must have come out at the smell of the cheese in the trap. In another few seconds it would have whisked to the trap to take the cheese, and— WHAM!—Andy would have been too late.

Andy stared at the mouse, and the mouse stared at Andy. Then Andy whispered, "Shoo!" and the mouse flickered and was gone.

Then Andy got down on hands and knees and poked at the cheese with his stick, and the spring released, and the snapper whammed down and the twig was broken. At the shock the cheese flew in fragments all over the larder floor. Then Andy picked up the two parts of the stick and put them back in the stick box.

He left the cheese where it was; the mouse would finish that. He left the mousetrap where it was. It was quite safe for tonight; but his father would want to reset it tomorrow night,

and Andy might be a few seconds late tomorrow night, and then the mouse would be dead.

He wished he dare take the mousetrap away and destroy it somehow, but he dared not.

He shut the larder door and crept upstairs to bed again.

In the morning Andy's father was very cross when he went to look in the larder. He said that the cheese had gone—every crumb of it. He didn't know how the mouse had managed it. It had taken the cheese, and the snapper had come down—and missed the mouse! The mouse had escaped.

"I'll set the trap in the same place tonight," said Andy's father. "And this time I'll catch that mouse."

Andy's father had picked up the mousetrap and put it on the table where everyone was busy getting together the things for today's walk and picnic. Someone in a hurry put a bag of sandwiches on top of the mousetrap, without noticing. Someone else added some apples and bananas. There were bottles of water and vacuum flasks. Bathing things and anoraks were gathered onto the table. The table was being piled with things for the excursion, and underneath them all was the mousetrap.

Andy saw his chance.

When no one was looking, Andy slid his hand under the piles of things and groped about until he felt the mousetrap. Very secretly he pulled the mousetrap out and put it into his pocket.

With the mousetrap in his pocket Andy strolled from the little old house into the sunshine outside. He strolled toward the stream. He reached a bush, behind which he would be quite out of sight of the house. The ground here was boggy, with clumps of moss like little bright green cushions. He lifted one of the cushions of moss and put the mousetrap underneath. He pressed the mousetrap down until brown bog water rose and seeped over it. Then he put the cushion of moss back on top. It did not look as if it had ever been disturbed, but underneath was the mousetrap. The wood of the mousetrap would rot in the bog water, and the metal of the mousetrap would rust away, and in the end THE EXECUTIONER would have gone forever.

Andy was glad that he had done what he did, but he was also afraid. He knew that his father would be very angry indeed if he ever found out. Andy's mother would be less angry. She hated mice, but she would understand why Andy had to save this one.

Anyway, they were not going to find out, Andy thought. And indeed, they never did.

Andy's father was very cross, all over again, when, later, he couldn't find his mousetrap. "I put it here on the table," he said. "Someone must have noticed it." But no one had.

(Except for me, thought Andy.)

Andy's father searched and searched. He even went through the dustbins. "It must be somewhere," he said. "It just must be *somewhere."*

(So it is, thought Andy.)

Finally Andy's father had to give up. "I simply don't know where it can have got to."

(But Andy knew.)

Andy's father would not buy another mousetrap because the first one might always turn up after all. And anyway, this was almost the end of the holiday.

On the last day of the holiday all the suit-cases and knapsacks and baskets and bags were packed up, and the holiday party was ready to leave the little old house to itself.

"Shall I see if anything's left in the larder?" said Andy.

Someone said at once that nothing could have been left there, but Andy was already at the larder door, opening it. The larder was quite empty, but on the other side, where the wall met the floor, was a little dark hole, mouse size.

"Goodbye!" Andy whispered to the hole, and then, "Good luck!"

Then Andy and his mother and father and aunt and uncle and cousins left the little old house, having locked the door and left the key under the mat for the next lot of holiday-makers. Until that new lot came, the little old house was left to itself, empty, still, and quiet.

Hello,
Polly!

Every summer the children's zoo came to the park.

Vicky loved to go to the zoo with her mother and her little brother, Johnny. This year they went again as usual.

As usual, there were goats and sheep and rabbits, fenced into separate enclosures, and there were Shetland ponies ready saddled for children to ride. But this year there was something quite new: a kind of huge metal caravan, painted blue.

"Whatever is it?" cried Vicky.

She ran around the caravan, ahead of her mother and Johnny, and came to the other side of it. Then she saw what it was. The other side of the caravan had doors that folded right back, so that you could see inside, and inside were three big cages. One cage had a squirrel in it, one cage had two monkeys in it, and the third cage had a parrot.

In all the cages there were perches and little ladders, and a great many cut branches with green leaves still on them. So the insides of the cages were green and jungly. The creatures in the cages climbed or leaped or swung, rustling among the leaves as they went. They made no other sound, except once when the

parrot spoke in a hoarse little voice. Vicky heard it speak. She was standing in front of the caravan cage with some other children when the parrot said, *"Hello, Polly!"*

At once the children in front of the cage called back, "Hello, Polly!" and also, "Hello—hello—hello—hello!" and even, "Goodbye, Polly!" Some of the children shouted to their friends to come and listen to the parrot. Soon there was a little crowd of children in front of the parrot's cage. They were calling to the parrot and to each other, and laughing, and jumping about with excitement: a noisy little crowd of children.

And all the time the parrot stood on its perch and stared at the noisy little crowd and never spoke again.

"Did the parrot really say, 'Hello, Polly!'?" asked Vicky's mother. She and Johnny had joined the crowd in front of the cages.

"Yes, it did. It really did. I heard it," said Vicky. "But it won't speak now." She was very disappointed.

They waited a little while, in case the parrot spoke again, but it didn't. Johnny began to fret. "I don't like parrots," he said. "I like ponies."

So they moved on to the ponies, and Vicky and Johnny each had a ride. Then they went to look at the goats and sheep and rabbits. Then Vicky wanted another pony ride, but her mother said, "No, Vicky. We must leave all the animals now. We're going to the other side of the park to have tea with Aunt Nora."

Vicky said, "But I want to stay at the zoo!"

"No, Vicky," said her mother. "We can come to the zoo again tomorrow. Today Aunt Nora is expecting us to tea."

"Bother Aunt Nora!" said Vicky.

"Now, Vicky!" said her mother. "You know Aunt Nora always has a special surprise for you both at tea, and you like that."

"I hate Aunt Nora," said Vicky, "and I hate her old tea!"

Vicky's mother set off across the park, pushing Johnny in his chair. Vicky had to follow. She was very cross. Vicky's mother said over her shoulder to Vicky, "Perhaps all the animals will still be there when we come back over the park after tea."

Vicky said, "I bet they won't be. I just bet they won't be."

They reached Aunt Nora's house, and she had tea ready for them in her little garden under the apple tree. She and Vicky's mother sat at one end of the garden table, having ordinary tea. At the other end Vicky and Johnny had doll's tea-party tea.

That was Aunt Nora's special surprise.

Aunt Nora had got out her own doll's tea set with tiny cups and saucers and plates that

she had played with when she was a little girl.
She had cut tiny sandwiches, some of peanut
butter, some of honey; each sandwich was no
bigger than a postage stamp. She had baked
tiny buns the size of marbles; and she had cut
each fish finger into four, so that it made doll's
fish fingers. There was real tea in a tiny teapot, and Vicky poured it because she was
older than Johnny.

Vicky loved the doll's tea party, and so did
Johnny.

After tea Vicky climbed the apple tree,
while Johnny sat on his mother's knee. She
climbed so high that she could see into the
park, but she couldn't see the children's zoo.
When she climbed down from the apple tree,
it was time to go home.

As they went home across the park, Vicky's
mother said to her, "I knew you'd enjoy tea
with Aunt Nora. You always do."

Vicky said, "I hope the animals will still be
there."

But they weren't. Even from a distance they
could see that the ponies had gone, and the
goats and the sheep and the rabbits. They had

all been taken away for the night by the children's zoo keepers. All the people had gone, too. The only things left were the fencing of the empty enclosures and the blue caravan. The caravan was shut up, and its doors were padlocked.

Vicky said sadly, "We're too late."

"Never mind," said her mother. "The animals will all be brought back again tomorrow. We can come and see them again tomorrow."

Now they were passing the enclosures, all quiet and lonely. Next they came to the caravan.

Johnny asked, "Do the zoo men live in that caravan?"

"No, dear," said his mother. "That was the caravan with the cages in it, with the squirrel and the monkeys and the parrot."

"Why can't the squirrel and the monkeys and the parrot still be in their cages in the caravan?" asked Johnny.

"No, dear," said his mother.

Vicky said, "But I don't see why not!"

"It's all shut up tight," said her mother. "How would the animals breathe?"

"There are those funny windows up there," said Vicky. There were slatted windows, high up under the roof of the caravan. "So they could breathe; they might still be inside."

"I suppose they might," said her mother.

They came close to the caravan and stood just below one of the windows and listened. There was only silence from inside the caravan. After a while their mother was going to say something, but Vicky whispered, "Hush!"

They listened. This time they thought they heard a rustling sound from inside the caravan. Then it stopped. Then—quite clearly—it started again, and went on for a little while.

"There is something inside," Vicky said in a whisper. "It's rustling the leaves on the branches inside the caravan."

"I really believe you're right," said her mother. She looked up at the slatted windows. "You're too heavy for me to hold, Vicky, but I could hold Johnny up to a window." So she held Johnny up.

He peered between the slats of the window. "It's dark inside," he said. Then he said, "I think something moved." But then his mother had to put him on the ground again because even he was too heavy to hold up for long.

But Vicky was determined to find out what was inside the caravan. She climbed onto the towbar, under one of the slatted windows, and stretched up, standing on tiptoe. She was still not quite high enough to see through the window, but she could hear well. She could hear a rustling of leaves. And suddenly she heard a hoarse little voice. *"Hello!"* it said, very quietly.

Vicky said to her mother and Johnny, "It's the parrot! Listen!" But there was no sound at all now. Then Vicky said, "Hello!" not very loudly, but just loudly enough to be heard inside the caravan.

Still silence.

Then she tried to imitate the parrot's own hoarse little voice. "Hello!" she said.

There was a pause. Then a hoarse little parrot voice answered, *"Hello, Polly!"*

"Hello!" said Vicky again.

"Hello!" said the little voice from inside the caravan, and there was a rustling of leaves, as

though the parrot were moving about. *"Hello, hello, hello!"* it said.

"I can talk to the parrot!" Vicky whispered to her mother and Johnny. "Listen!" And she used her parrot-speaking voice again. "Hello, Polly!"

Another pause, and then a little voice answered, *"Hello, hello!"*

Vicky whispered, "I expect he's lonely inside there, in the dark, with only the squirrel and the monkeys for company. They don't talk to him, but I can talk to him." So she did. "Hello, Polly!"

"Hello!" replied the parrot.

Vicky's mother said, "He'll like it better in the morning, when the zoo men bring all the other animals back and open up the caravan again." She and Johnny tried calling "Hello!" to the parrot, but it wouldn't answer. Either it didn't hear them, or they didn't say "Hello!" in the way it liked.

"Hello, Polly!" said Vicky, for the umpteenth time.

"Hello!" said the parrot.

"Hello!" said Vicky.

"Hello!" said the parrot.

"We must really go now," said Vicky's mother. She had said this before, and this time Vicky had to pay attention.

"See you tomorrow, Polly!" Vicky called softly through the slatted window. "Goodbye, Polly!"

"Hello, Polly!" said the parrot because that was the most it could say.

"Goodbye!" said Vicky, one last time. She climbed down from the towbar to where the others were waiting for her.

Then Vicky and her mother and her little brother, Johnny, went home from the park.

The
Manatee

The first time that Totty slept away from home was when he went to stay with his grandfather for one night. He went with his elder sister; they slept in two separate beds in the same bedroom. That night Totty didn't feel at all homesick. After all, he had his sister.

Then Totty went all by himself to spend a night with his grandfather. He had said he wanted to do that.

On that visit, in the afternoon, Totty and his grandfather went to the park together, and Totty's grandfather pushed him high on the swings. Then they came home and had tea with baked beans and ice cream afterward.

After tea Totty's grandfather got out a book of wild animal pictures to show him. Totty's best animals were fierce lions and tigers and jaguars and ravening wolves. Almost at the end of the book there was a picture of two dark gray creatures lolling in the shallow water of some strange river. They had heavy heads and tiny eyes and huge, bristling upper lips. Their forelegs looked rather like canoe paddles, and Totty couldn't see any back legs at all.

"They're fish," said Totty.

"No," said his grandfather. "They're not fish. They're animals called manatees. It says so here."

Totty stared at the manatees in the picture and thought. Then he asked, "What do manatees eat?"

But either his grandfather did not want to answer that question, or he did not hear it—he was an old man and rather deaf. He shut the animal book with a snap and said, "Time for bed, young Totty!"

So Totty went to bed.

He slept in the same bedroom as before, but of course, the other bed in it was empty this time. All the same, it had been properly made up with a pillow and sheets and blankets. This was in case Totty's sister had come, too.

Totty's grandfather said goodnight to Totty and turned off the bedroom light. He left the bedroom door a little ajar, so that Totty could see the light on the landing outside.

Totty heard his grandfather go downstairs, and then he heard the sound of television. His grandfather would probably watch television all evening.

Totty did not go to sleep. He didn't feel lonely, but all the same, he thought it would have been nice to have someone sleeping in the other bed. After a while he got up and went out onto the landing, where it was light. He looked down the stairs. The stairs were painted white, with a narrow brown carpet coming up the middle of them. Totty wasn't used to stairs; his family lived in a flat.

After a while he went back into his bedroom, closing the door again so that it was a little ajar, as before. When he had opened the door to go onto the landing, and now when he almost closed it, the hinges had creaked. Totty's grandfather had already said they needed a spot of oil. He had said this was a little job that Totty and he could do tomorrow morning.

Totty got back into bed, and this time he began to go to sleep. Suddenly he was wide-awake again because his grandfather had turned off the television set. Now he could hear his grandfather locking up the house, get-

ting ready to go to bed. His grandfather
turned out all the lights. He went to bed.

Now there was no light from the landing,
shining through the narrow opening of Totty's
door. Everything was dark.

Totty lay awake. He couldn't see anything,
but after a while he thought he had heard
something. He thought he heard a tiny, soft

little sound like a *flop* on the stairs—far down, at the bottom of the stairs.

Had he heard it, or hadn't he?

There was no one but himself and his grandfather in the house, so there just couldn't be a person creeping up the stairs.

All the same, he became almost sure that there was someone or something at the bottom of his grandfather's stairs, just beginning to climb them.

He held his breath so that he could listen as carefully as possible, and he shut his eyes, too. As soon as he shut his eyes, he saw quite clearly what it was at the bottom of the stairs, preparing to come up them. It was a manatee.

The manatee had lifted its bristly face and was looking with its beady eyes toward the landing upstairs. It had put one of its forelegs on the bottom step of the stairs, and now—a heave of its great gray weight, and it was up the first step.

Totty opened his eyes, and then he couldn't see the manatee on the stairs anymore. He could see only the darkness. He couldn't hear the manatee either, but that was because he had to breathe and his heart had to beat, and the sound of his own breathing and the beating of his own heart covered the very slight, soft sound that even the most cunning manatee would have to make as it came upstairs.

Totty said to himself: *If I yell and yell, Grandfather will wake up and hear me and come. I'll tell him there's a manatee on the stairs, and he'll go and look and say there's nothing there. Then he'll go back to bed, and I shall lie here in the dark again, all by myself, and the manatee will start coming up the stairs all over again.*

So Totty didn't call to his grandfather—yet.

He didn't make any noise at all that might stop his hearing the manatee coming up the stairs. He breathed as quietly as he could, and he didn't move any part of his body, to make even the smallest rustle of the sheets.

The manatee must be reaching the top of the stairs by now.

Totty tried to lie still and silent as a stone.

Now the manatee would be snuffling around the landing. It found Totty's bedroom door ajar. It didn't find his door by accident; the manatee was looking for it. It had known that Totty's door would be ajar.

Now, Totty thought, *if the manatee pushes the door wider open to come in, the hinges will creak. If the hinges creak, the manatee is coming in.*

But the manatee did not push the door wider open. Instead, it began to make itself thin. Totty knew why the manatee was making itself thin. It made itself thinner and thinner, until at last it was thin enough to slide through the crack of the door into Totty's bedroom.

Now, thought Totty, *the manatee is going to rear up at the foot of the bed. The manatee is a man-eater. It wants to eat* me. *So yell—yell— YELL—*

Totty tried to open his mouth to yell for his grandfather, but his mouth wouldn't open. His teeth, clamped together, kept it shut. In vain he struggled and struggled to open his mouth and yell. As he tried, he thought desperately: *Suppose I could* persuade *the manatee not to eat me? Suppose I could persuade it that there was something else that it would be nicer to do?*

Totty was thinking hard, and he thought

one thing, and the manatee waiting at the foot of his bed listened to Totty's thought. It paid attention. The manatee began to heave itself slowly, slowly across the bedroom floor from Totty's bed to the other bed, which was empty. Slowly, slowly—with Totty thinking hard all the time—the manatee heaved itself up onto the bed. Very carefully indeed, so as not to disturb the bedclothes by a rumple or even a wrinkle, it slipped into the bed between the sheets.

Inside his head Totty heard the manatee say *Ah!* in a deep, bristly voice. Then it said: *How beautifully comfortable!* Then it fell fast asleep.

Totty waited a little while until he was sure the manatee was asleep. Then he went to sleep, too.

He felt quite safe.

When Totty woke in the morning, the manatee had gone. In going, it had not marked the cleanness of the sheets on the other bed or disturbed its smoothness.

Totty went down to breakfast with his grandfather. He asked him a question about manatees. His grandfather fetched the book of animal pictures and found the right page. He read what the book said about Manatees.

"'They are slow in their movements,'" read Grandfather.

"Yes," said Totty.

"'And perfectly harmless.'"

"Not man-eating?" said Totty.

"No. It says here that they are vegetarian. They eat only water weeds. They live in water."

"They never come right out onto dry land and into houses?"

"Never?"

Totty was disappointed. He would have

liked to have spent another night in his grand-father's house with the manatee sleeping in the bed next to his. It would have been a friendly, comfortable thing to do.

But you couldn't expect a water animal to heave itself up a staircase and into a bed night after night, even to please a friend. Totty knew that. Once would have to be enough.

The Crooked Little Finger

One morning Judy woke up with a funny feeling in her little finger. It didn't exactly hurt, but it was beginning to ache, and it was beginning to itch. It felt wrong. She held it straight out, and it still felt wrong. She curved it in on itself, with all the other fingers, and it still felt wrong.

In the end she got dressed and went down to breakfast, holding that little finger straight up in the air, quite separately.

She sat down to breakfast and said to her mother and her father and to her big brother, David, and her young sister, Daisy, "My little finger's gone wrong."

David asked, "What have you done to it?"

"Nothing," said Judy. "I just woke up this morning, and it somehow felt wrong."

Her mother said, "I expect you'll wake up tomorrow morning and it'll somehow feel right."

"What about today, though?" asked Judy, but her mother wasn't listening anymore.

Her father said, "You haven't broken a bone in your little finger, have you, Judy? Can you bend it? Can you crook it—like this—as though you were beckoning with it?"

"Yes," said Judy, and then, *"Ooooow!"*

"Did it hurt then?" said her mother, suddenly listening again, and anxious.

"No," said Judy. "It didn't hurt at all when I crooked it. But it felt *very* funny. It felt wrong. I didn't like it."

David said, "I'm tired of Judy's little finger," and their mother said, "Forget your little finger, Judy, and get on with your breakfast."

So Judy stopped talking about her little finger, but she couldn't forget it. It felt so odd. She tried crooking it again and discovered that it wanted to crook itself. That was what it had been aching to do and itching to do.

She crooked it while she poured milk on her cereal and then waited for David to finish with the sugar.

Suddenly—

"Hey!" David cried angrily. "Don't *do* that, Judy!"

"What is it now?" exclaimed their mother, startled.

"She snatched the sugar from under my nose, just when I was helping myself." He was still holding the sugar spoon up in the air.

"I didn't!" said Judy.

"You did!" said David. "How else did the sugar get from me to you like that?"

"I crooked my little finger at it," said Judy.

David said, "What rubbish!" and their mother said, "Pass the sugar back to David at once, Judy."

Their father said nothing but stared at Judy's little finger, and Daisy said, "The sugar went quick through the air. I saw it." But nobody paid any attention to Daisy, of course.

Judy began to say, "My little finger—"

But her mother interrupted her. "Judy, we don't want to hear any more at all about that little finger. There's nothing wrong with it."

So Judy said no more at all about her little finger, but went on feeling very wrong.

Her father was the first to go, off to work. He kissed his wife goodbye, and his baby daughter, Daisy. He said, "Be a good boy!" to David, and he said, "Be a good girl!" to Judy. Then he stooped and kissed Judy, as he didn't usually do in the morning rush, and he whispered in her ear, "Watch out for that little finger of yours that wants to be crooked!"

Then he went off to work, and a little later Judy and David went off to school.

And Judy's little finger still felt wrong, aching and itching in its strange way.

Judy sat in her usual place in the classroom, listening to Mrs. Potter reading a story aloud. While she listened, Judy looked around the classroom and caught sight of an india rubber she had often seen before and wished were hers. The india rubber was shaped and colored just like a perfect little pink pig with a roving eye. It belonged to a boy called Simon, whom she didn't know very well. Even if they had known each other very well indeed, he probably wouldn't have wanted to give Judy his perfect pink pig india rubber.

As it was, Judy just stared at the india rubber and longed to have it. While she longed, her little finger began to ache very much indeed and to itch very much indeed. It ached and itched to be allowed to crook itself, to beckon.

In the end Judy crooked her little finger.

Then there was a tiny sound like a puff of breath, and something came sailing through the air from Simon's table to Judy's table, and

it landed with a little *flop!* just by Judy's hand. And Mrs. Potter had stopped reading the story and was crying, "Whatever are you doing, Simon Smith, to be throwing india rubbers about? We don't throw india rubbers about in this classroom!"

"I didn't throw my india rubber!" said Simon. He was very much flustered.

"Then how does it happen to be here?" Mrs. Potter had come over to Judy's table to pick up the india rubber. She turned it over, and there was SIMON SMITH written in ink on the underside.

Simon said nothing; and of course, Judy said nothing; and Mrs. Potter said, "We *never* throw india rubbers about in this classroom, Simon. I shall put this india rubber up on my desk, and there it stays until the dinner break."

But it didn't stay there—oh, no! Judy waited and waited until no one in the classroom—no one at all—was looking, and then she crooked her little finger, and the india rubber came sailing through the air again—*flop!* onto her table, just beside her. This time Judy picked it up very quickly and quietly and put it into her pocket.

At the end of the morning Simon went up to Mrs. Potter's desk to get his india rubber back again, and it wasn't there. He searched round about, and so did Mrs. Potter, but they couldn't find the india rubber. In the end Mrs. Potter was bothered and cross, and Simon was crying. They had no idea where the india rubber could have got to.

But Judy knew exactly where it was.

Now Judy knew what her little finger could do—what it ached and itched to be allowed to do. But she didn't want anyone else to know what it could do. That would have spoiled everything. She would have had to return Simon's pink pig india rubber and anything else her little finger crooked itself to get.

So she was very, very careful. At dinnertime she managed to crook her little finger at a second helping of syrup pudding, when no one was looking, and she got it and ate it. Later on she crooked her little finger at the prettiest seashell on the nature table, and no one saw it come through the air to her, and she put it into her pocket with the pink pig india rubber. Later still she crooked her finger at another girl's hair ribbon, which was hanging loose, and at a useful two-colored pencil.

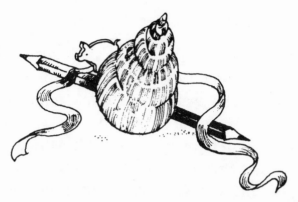

By the end of the school day the pocket with the pink pig india rubber was crammed full of things which did not belong to Judy but which had come to her when she crooked her little finger.

And what did Judy feel like? Right in the middle of her—in her stomach—she felt a heaviness because she had eaten too much syrup pudding.

In her head, at the very top of her head, there was a fizziness of airy excitement that made her feel almost giddy.

And somewhere between the top of her head and her stomach she felt uncomfortable. She wanted to think about all the things hidden in her pocket and to enjoy the thought, but on the other hand, she didn't want to think about them at all. Especially she didn't want to think about Simon Smith crying for his pink pig india rubber. The wanting to think and the *not* wanting to think made her feel very uncomfortable indeed.

When school was over, Judy went home with her brother, David, as usual. They were passing the sweetshop, not far from their home, when Judy said, "I'd like some chocolate or some toffees."

"You haven't any money to buy chocolate or toffees," said David. "Nor have I. Come on, Judy."

Judy said, "Daisy once went in there, and the shopman gave her a toffee. She hadn't any money, and he *gave* her a toffee."

"That's because she was so little—a baby, really," said David. "He wouldn't give you a toffee if you hadn't money to buy it."

"It's not fair," said Judy. And her little finger felt as if it agreed with her. It ached and it itched, and it longed to crook itself. But Judy wouldn't let it—yet. She and David passed the sweetshop and went on home to tea.

After tea it grew dark outside. Indoors everyone was busy, except for Judy. Her mother was bathing Daisy and putting her to bed; her father was mending something; David was making an airplane out of numbered parts. Nobody was noticing Judy, so she slipped out of the house and went along the street to the sweetshop.

It was quite dark by now, except for the streetlamps. All the shops were shut; there was nobody about. Judy would have been frightened to be out alone, after dark, without anyone's knowing, but her little finger ached and her little finger itched, and she could think of nothing else.

She reached the sweetshop and looked in through the window. There were pretty tins of toffee and chocolate boxes tied with bright ribbon on display in the window. She peered beyond them, to the back of the shop, where she could just see the bars of chocolate stacked like bricks and the rows of big jars of boiled sweets and the packets and cartons and tubes of sweets and toffees and chocolates and other delightful things that she could only guess at in the dimness of the inside of the shop.

And Judy crooked her little finger.

She held her little finger crooked, and she saw the bars of chocolate and the jars of boiled sweets and all the other things beginning to move from the back of the shop toward the front, toward the window. Soon the window was crowded close with sweets of all kinds pressing against the glass, as though they had come to stare at her and at her crooked little finger. Judy backed away from the shop-window, to the other side of the street; but she still held her little finger crooked, and all the things in the sweetshop pressed up against the

window and pressed and crowded and pressed and pressed, harder and harder, against the glass of the shopwindow, until—CRACK! The window shattered, and everything in it came flying out toward Judy as she stood there with her little finger crooked.

She was so frightened that she turned and ran for home as fast as she could, and behind her she heard a hundred thousand things from the sweetshop come skittering and skidding and bumping and thumping along the pavement after her.

She ran and she ran and she reached her front gate and then her front door and she ran in through the front door and slammed it shut behind her and heard all the things that had been chasing her come rattling and banging

against the front door and then fall to the ground.

Then she found that she had uncrooked her little finger.

Although she was safe now, Judy ran upstairs to her bedroom and flung herself upon her bed and cried. As she lay there, crying, she held her little finger out straight in front of her and said to it, "I hate you—I HATE you!"

From her bed she began to hear shouts and cries and the sound of running feet in the street outside, and her father's voice, and then her mother's, as they went out to see what had happened. There were people talking and talking, their voices high and loud with excitement and amazement. Later there was the sound of a police car coming, and more talk.

But in the end the noise and the excitement died away, and at last everything was quiet. Then she heard footsteps on the stairs, and her bedroom door opened, and her father's voice said, "Are you there, Judy?"

"Yes."

He came in and sat down on her bed. He said that her mother was settling Daisy, so he had come to tell her what had been happening. He said there had been a smash-and-grab raid at the sweetshop. There must have been a whole gang of raiders, and they had got clean away; no one had seen them. But the gang had had to dump their loot in their hurry to escape. They had thrown it all—chocolates and toffees and sweets and everything—into the first convenient front garden. Judy's father said that the stuff had all been flung into their own front garden and against their own front door.

As she listened, Judy wept and wept. Her father did not ask her why she was crying, but at last he said, "How is that little finger?"

Judy said, "I hate it!"

"I daresay," said her father. "But does it ache and itch anymore?"

Judy thought a moment. "No," she said, "it doesn't." She stopped crying.

"Judy," said her father, "if it ever starts aching and itching again, *don't crook it.*"

"I won't," said Judy. "I never will again. Never. Ever."

The next day Judy went early to school,

even before David. When she got into the classroom, only Mrs. Potter was there, at the teacher's desk.

Judy went straight to the teacher's desk and brought out from her pocket the pink pig india rubber and the shell and the hair ribbon and the two-color pencil and all the other things. She put them on Mrs. Potter's desk, and Mrs. Potter looked at them and said nothing.

Judy said, "I'm sorry. I'm really and truly sorry. And my father says to tell you that I had a crooked little finger yesterday. But it won't crook itself again, ever. I shan't let it."

"I've heard of crooked little fingers," said Mrs. Potter. "In the circumstances, Judy, we'll say no more."

And Judy's little finger never crooked itself again, ever.

The Great
Sharp Scissors

Once there was a boy called Tim who was often naughty. Then his mother used to say, *"Tim!"* and his father shouted, "TIM!" But his granny always said, "Tim's a good boy, really." Tim loved his granny very much. He went to visit her often, and when he went, his granny always gave him a special present.

One day Tim's mother had a message that his granny was ill. She decided to go to her at once, and Tim said, "I'll come, too."

"No, you can't come," said his mother. "Granny's too ill."

Tim scowled and stamped his foot. He was very angry.

"You'll have to stay at home by yourself," said his mother. "You'll have to be good. I won't be long."

Tim said nothing. He just scowled and scowled.

"And if the front door bell rings, Tim, you're not to let any stranger in the house." Then his mother hurried off.

Tim shut the front door, and then he just stood, feeling angrier than he had ever felt before. He listened to his mother's footsteps hurrying down the front path, out through the front gate, and along the street. When he could no longer hear them, he heard other footsteps coming along the street, in at the front gate, and up the front path to the front door. Then the bell rang.

Tim just stood.

The bell rang again.

Still Tim stood.

Then the flap of the letter box went up, and two eyes looked through. A voice—a strange man's voice—called through the letter box, "Tim, aren't you going to let me in?"

Tim decided what to do. He went to the

door, and he put the chain on it, and then he opened the door; but the chain prevented its opening wide enough for anyone to get in. Tim peered through the gap of the door and saw a strange man on the doorstep with a suitcase in his hand.

"I have things here that you might like," said the stranger. He laid his suitcase flat on the doorstep and opened it.

First of all Tim saw a notice inside, and this is what it said:

| WE |
| SELL |
| KNIVES |
| SCISSORS |
| BATTLE-AXES |

"I'd like a battle-ax," said Tim.

"We're out of battle-axes at the moment," said the stranger.

"Knives?" said Tim.

"Yes," said the stranger. "But what about scissors? I have a most remarkable pair of great sharp scissors." He reached into the suitcase and brought out an enormous pair of scissors. The blades shone sharp and dangerously. "They'll cut anything," said the stranger. *"Anything."*

"I'll have them," said Tim, and he held out his hand.

"Ah," said the stranger, "but you can't have something for nothing. You must pay for these very valuable scissors."

"Wait there," said Tim. He ran and fetched his money box. He reached his hand through the gap of the door and gave the stranger all the money from his money box. In return, the stranger gave Tim the pair of great sharp scissors. Then he smiled at Tim in a way Tim did not like and went away.

Tim shut the front door and looked at the scissors in his hand. He clashed the blades together and remembered how angry he was. He decided to try the scissors out at once. The stranger had said they would cut anything. *Anything.*

He saw his father's coat hanging in the hall. With his scissors he cut off all the buttons of his father's coat. *Snip! Snap! Snip! Snap!* The buttons all fell to the floor. It was very easy.

But of course, even an ordinary pair of scissors would cut the buttons off a coat. Tim went into the living room to find something

more difficult for the great sharp scissors. He
would try them on the carpet.

With his scissors he cut the carpet in two—
Snip! Snap! Just like that. Then he cut it again
and again and again. He snipped and snapped
at the carpet with his great sharp scissors until
he had cut it into hundreds of little pieces.

Then Tim tried cutting the wooden leg off a chair. *Snip! Snap!* The great sharp scissors snipped the wooden leg off the chair, just like that. Then Tim snipped the legs off all the chairs and off the table. He cut the sofa in two. *Snip! Snap!*

He tried the great sharp scissors on the clock on the mantelpiece. The blades went through the metal and glass very easily. *Snip! Snap!* And the clock was in half.

He thought he would cut his goldfish in its goldfish bowl, but then he felt sorry for the goldfish. So he took it out and put it safely into the handbasin full of water. Then he did cut the goldfish bowl with his great sharp scissors. The blades went through the glass without even splintering it. *Snip! Snap!* Just like that. And the water from the goldfish bowl went all over the floor.

By now Tim knew that his great sharp scissors would cut anything. They would cut through the floors and the wooden doors. They would cut through all the bricks of the walls. They would cut through the slates of the roof. They would cut his whole home into a heap of rubble, and they had begun to do so.

Tim went and sat on the bottom step of the stairs and cried.

Presently he heard footsteps. They came along the street, in at the front gate, and up the front path to the front door. Then the bell rang.

Tim was very frightened. He was afraid that the same strange man had come back. He sat absolutely still, absolutely quiet.

The bell rang again.

Still Tim sat.

Then the flap of the letter box went up, and two eyes looked through. A voice—a strange woman's voice—called through the letter box, "Tim, aren't you going to open the door a little?"

So Tim opened the door on the chain again and looked out. On the doorstep stood a

strange woman with a lidded basket on her
arm. She smiled kindly at Tim and lifted the
lid of her basket.

First of all Tim saw a notice inside, and this
is what it said:

> BUY
>
> GLUES
>
> INSTANT
>
> INVISIBLE
>
> UNBREAKABLE

Tim said, "I've been using a pair of great sharp scissors. I've made an awful, awful mess of everything." He cried again.

The woman said, "I think you need my very best spray-on glue."

"Yes, please," said Tim, and he held out his hand.

"Ah," said the woman, "but you can't have something for nothing, can you?"

Tim said, "I've no money at all. I used it all to buy the scissors."

"I tell you what," said the woman, "you let me have those expensive scissors, and I'll let you have my best glue in exchange. You spray the glue round about, and it sticks things together instantly, just as they were before."

So Tim gave the woman the great sharp scissors, and she gave him the glue. Then she went off, and he shut the door and took the chain off.

He thought he would try the glue out first on his father's coat. It worked. He sprayed all the buttons back on, as if they had never been cut off.

He went into the living room, and he

sprayed all the little pieces of carpet back together again, so that there was one whole carpet again. He sprayed the legs back onto all
the chairs and the table. He sprayed the sofa
together again. He sprayed the two halves of
the clock together again, and at once it began
ticking again.

He sprayed the goldfish bowl together
again—but of course, the water was still on
the floor. Tim refilled the bowl with water and
put the goldfish back.

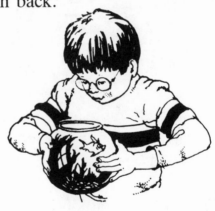

He'd just got everything straight when he
heard the sound of a key in the front door
lock; his mother was home.

His mother walked in, smiling.

She said, "Granny's much better and sends her love." She looked around. "I see you've been a good boy, Tim. Everything's still spick-and-span."

Tim said, "The goldfish water is all over the floor."

"Accidents will happen," said his mother. "I'll mop it up." While she mopped it up, she told Tim that his granny had sent him a special present. "She made it for you a long time ago," said Tim's mother. "She told me to take it from her store cupboard." And Tim's mother brought out from her bag a pot of homemade raspberry jam, which was Tim's favorite jam.

Then Tim's mother made a pot of tea, and she and Tim had tea and new bread and butter and raspberry jam. In the middle of it, Tim's father came home, and he had some of the raspberry jam, too.

Secrets

The Barker family had been out for a day in the country, and now they were beginning to drive home.

"We'll stop for tea if we see anywhere," said Mrs. Barker, but at first they didn't see anywhere. The four children squeezed on the back seat of the car began to grumble. They were hungry and thirsty, and all of them wanted to go to the toilet, except for Shirley. "We can't wait," they said.

Then the Barkers saw a notice ahead of them: TEAS.

Mrs. Barker cried, "Stop!" to Mr. Barker, and he slowed the car to a stop at the notice.

They all looked past the notice, up a garden path to the front door of a long, low thatched cottage. The door of the cottage stood open, and a little boy sat on the threshold in the afternoon sun. He was sucking his thumb. A white cat slid around his ankles, rubbing itself against them.

"Hello, Suck-a-thumb!" Mr. Barker called. "Tell your mum we're coming in for tea!"

The little boy got up, without taking his thumb from his mouth, and went indoors. The cat followed him. The two of them vanished into the darkness of the inside of the cottage. The door was left open.

The Barkers climbed out of their car and went up the garden path and in through the open doorway. They found themselves at once in the tearoom, empty of other visitors. They chose the biggest table and sat down.

They looked around them. The tearoom had a low ceiling and walls with bulges and unexpected nooks. It was very old and surprisingly large. Mr. Barker said it must have been two rooms at some time, and the two rooms had been knocked into one. It had two doors, besides the door they had come in by, but one of these doors was blocked off by a table neatly stacked with clean white cups and saucers and plates. Through the other door, at the other end of the room, a woman now

came to take their order for tea. Suck-a-thumb came with her, but not the cat.

This must be the mother of Suck-a-thumb. As she stood talking to Mrs. Barker, he hid behind her and peeped out at the Barker children.

The Barker children, in order of age, were Wendy, Bill, Nicky, and Shirley. Suck-a-thumb stared and stared at them all. Wendy tried smiling at him, and Bill winked, and Nicky made faces; but Suck-a-thumb just went on sucking his thumb and staring. Shirley, who was the youngest of the Barker children, stared back.

Suck-a-thumb's mother took the order for tea and explained to Mrs. Barker where the toilet was, and then went off. Suck-a-thumb went with her.

There was the usual muddle of the Barkers all getting up to take off their anoraks and then sitting down again, and then getting up again to go to the toilet, and each person

going and then coming back, and then it was the next person's turn, and so on.

At last they were all sitting around the table again, waiting for their tea. Then Wendy said, "Mum, Shirley never went to the toilet."

"You never went?" cried her mother.

"I don't need to."

"I've heard that before! You go at once."

"Must I?"

"Yes. Remember: first right, first left, first right. Then the door's straight in front of you."

"Shirley doesn't know her right from her left," said Wendy.

"Shirley'll get lost," said Bill, and Nicky sniggered.

"I shan't," said Shirley. "First right, first left, first right. Then the door straight in front of me."

"Would you like Wendy to go with you?" said her mother.

"No."

Shirley went, murmuring the way to herself: *Right, left, right, the door straight in front of me, right, left, right, the door straight in front of me . . .*

She went out of the door from the tearoom
into a passage so dark that she felt frightened.
She wished she weren't alone after all. The
passage had furniture along one side, and she
edged past it. Then she came to a lighter passage to the left, so she turned down it.

Then she turned right.

Then she turned left again.

There was a door straight ahead of her, at the end of the last passage. This ought to be the door to the toilet, and yet somehow Shirley doubted that it was. She opened the door and found herself looking into the kitchen of the cottage. The air was warm and smelled deliciously of baking. On the kitchen table stood two wire racks. One was piled with fresh scones; the other with jam tarts. There was nobody in the kitchen except for Suck-a-thumb and the white cat. The cat was licking the last drops of milk from a saucer on the floor. Suck-a-thumb leaned against the corner of the table. For once his thumb was not in his mouth because he was eating a jam tart. He stared at Shirley and went on eating.

Shirley came a little way into the kitchen. She knew she ought to ask someone the way to the toilet. It would be no use asking Suck-a-thumb, but what about his mother? She could see that a scullery led off the kitchen, and she could hear taps running and somebody at work there. That would be Suck-a-thumb's mother.

Shirley knew she ought to go into the scullery and ask Suck-a-thumb's mother the way to the toilet, but she didn't want to.

Meanwhile, Suck-a-thumb seemed to have made up his mind to something. He stopped staring at Shirley and turned to the table behind him. He picked out a jam tart with one hand. Then with the other hand—but holding the glistening suck thumb well out of the way—he rearranged the remaining tarts so that no gap showed where a jam tart had been taken. No one would know.

He offered the jam tart to Shirley.

She was too surprised to speak. She took the tart and began eating it. The pastry was warm and crumbly; the jam was still hot.

She forgot about asking the way to the toilet. After all, she didn't need to go anyway.

The cat had finished its milk, and now it walked past Shirley and out through the door she had left open behind her. Suck-a-thumb moved his eyes from Shirley to the cat and back again. He beckoned to Shirley. He started after the cat, and Shirley followed him out of the kitchen. She closed the door quietly behind her.

In the dim passage Shirley could see the shape of Suck-a-thumb going ahead of her and the pale blur of the white cat ahead of him.

They turned two corners, and by now the white cat had disappeared. They stopped at a place where an old chair stood against a door. The chair had a broken back, and Shirley saw that its padded seat had fallen right through its seat frame. Someone had thrown a piece of

sacking partly over the seat frame, and this
sacking drooped around the sides of the chair
to the floor, like curtaining.

Suck-a-thumb lifted a corner of the sacking,
and Shirley saw the face of the white cat looking at her from a bed of seat stuffing and other
soft rags and rubbish. Around the cat there
were little movements, little cries.

"Kittens!" Shirley gave an exclamation of
delight, and at once Suck-a-thumb had put a

finger to his lips, to hush her. He managed to
do this without taking his thumb from his
mouth.

Shirley crouched down by the chair and reached under it, gently to touch the kittens. She stroked each one with the back of a finger; she whispered to them. The mother cat did not seem to mind. At last she dared pick a kitten up and bring it out from its secret home, and still the mother cat was purring.

Clasping a kitten, Shirley stood up. Now she began to notice sounds—distant, not loud, but somehow familiar. There were voices she thought she recognized.

She looked at Suck-a-thumb, and he was watching her intently. He laid his free hand against the door behind the broken chair, to draw her attention to it. The door looked quite out of use: the cracks all round it were stuffed with old newspaper. There was even a twist of newspaper in the keyhole, to stop the draft.

Suck-a-thumb took that twist of newspaper out and leaned past the broken chair to look through the keyhole. He did it all very neatly, Shirley thought, as if he had done it often before.

Then Suck-a-thumb moved aside, so that Shirley could look in her turn.

Shirley put the kitten back safely with its mother and brothers and sisters in their hiding place and looked through the keyhole.

At first she saw only strange white shapes, curved and shiny, that seemed to be just at the level of the keyhole and near it. Then, through a gap between these shapes, she was looking into the tearoom, straight at the table where her family sat. Suck-a-thumb's mother had just come into the tearoom carrying a tray loaded with scones and jam tarts and a big teapot and milk and sugar. It all went onto the Barkers' table.

Then Suck-a-thumb's mother scared Shirley. She came straight over toward her and stretched out her hands, so that they seemed as though they were reaching toward Shirley's eye at the keyhole. But the hands began to pick up some of the white shiny things Shirley had seen. There was a chinking of china. Then Shirley realized that the hands were picking up cups and saucers and plates. This was the china she had seen on the table in front of the disused door in the tearoom. She was looking through the keyhole of that same door.

Now Suck-a-thumb's mother was laying the extra china on the Barkers' tea table. Then she went out. The Barkers started their tea and began to talk among themselves. Shirley could hear them quite clearly, as well as watch them through the keyhole.

Her mother was saying, "Where *has* Shirley got to!"

"She got lost on the way to the toilet," said Bill.

"And on the way back," said Nicky.

"Wendy," said her mother, "wouldn't you like to go and hurry Shirley up?"

"In a minute," said Wendy, with her mouth full.

"You're not to eat everything up before the girl gets back," said Mr. Barker.

Mrs. Barker began putting scones and tarts on a plate. "This is Shirley's share."

Bill said, "When she comes, let's pretend we've eaten everything. Hide her plate under the table."

Wendy said, "I'll have it on my knees under the table."

"Yes—oh, yes!"

Shirley, with her eye at the keyhole, could have gone on watching them, listening to them forever. It was much more interesting than television.

But Suck-a-thumb was pulling at her to come away. She left the keyhole, and he stuffed the twist of newspaper back into place. No one would guess that the keyhole was ever used.

He waited while Shirley whispered goodbye to the cat and her kittens. Then he led the way back down passageways and around corners. He left her at the door of the tearoom.

She walked into the tearoom, and Wendy and Bill and Nicky all shouted at her, "You've been so long, we've had tea! We've eaten everything! There's nothing left!"

"Yes, there is," said Shirley. "Mum's kept a plate of scones and jam tarts for me. It's under the table. It's on Wendy's knees."

They goggled at her. They asked her again and again how she had guessed, but Shirley told them nothing.

After Mr. Barker had paid for their teas, they all trooped out to the car. Before they drove off, they looked up the garden path again. The cottage door stood open, and Suck-a-thumb sat on the doorstep, stroking the white cat.

They waved goodbye to him. Without taking his thumb out of his mouth, he waved back. It seemed as if he waved to all of them, but Shirley was certain that he waved to her.

They were halfway home when Shirley said, "I need to go to the toilet."

"No!" cried her mother. "You've just been, at that tea place. You can't want to go again!"

"I do."

"It beats me how they manage it," said Mr. Barker. He had begun to drive faster, in the hope of getting Shirley home in time. "It's a mystery to me," he said. "Just a mystery."

Shirley said nothing.